My friends the Flowers

By William Lach illustrated by Doug Kennedy

Abrams Books for Young Readers
New York

I love to visit with my friends,

my friends who are the flowers,
In country fields, suburban streets,
or shining city towers.
Annual, perennial, shrub, or tree,
Each flower-friend is full of fun and personality.

Marigold SCARES all the bugs.
He likes to make them run.

Sunflower's **big** happy face basks in the morning sun.

Morning Glory loves sun, too, and grows and grows and grows and grows.

I know of no one *prettier*—
or *pricklier*—than Rose.

Hollyhock is tall and slim.
She likes to dress in black.

Snapdragon is Spicy-Sweet
and eager to attack.

Daffodil will nod his head,
though always slightly **BENT**.

Camellia can be *gorgeous*,
but she doesn't have a scent.

Red Maple wears a veil of red,
quite early and quite faint.

Cornelian Cherry's yellow veil
takes on a greenish taint.

Hellebore will play alone out on the **snowy** ground.

Poppy's dress is **pretty**,
but she doesn't stick around.

Sweet Bay Magnolia's lemony,

but never, ever **sour**.

Four-O'Clocks are *bright* and **bold**,
though not before that hour.

Apple Blossom loves the bees
and gives the breezes **honey**.

But Cherry is Miss Popular as soon as spring gets sunny.

Prickly Pear can give a **SCARE** until you get to know him.

Azalea wears a shirt so bright
it almost seems to GLOW him.

Forsythia goes everywhere

to shake

her yellow bells.

And Miss Mock Orange sings as *sweet* as her old nickname tells.

Nicotiana wears her perfume

when the sun goes

DOWN.

Impatiens brothers hang around
the **shady** parts of town.

Tall Tulip Tree holds flowers high,
and then she lets them fall.

Franklinia's a late bloomer
and ʀᴀʀᴇꜱᴛ of them all.

Flowers grow most **everywhere**,

from cactus plant to tree,

And on the ground or *in the air,* my friends are good to see.
I love my friends so very much. They very much love me.

I love my friends especially because
I am a bee!

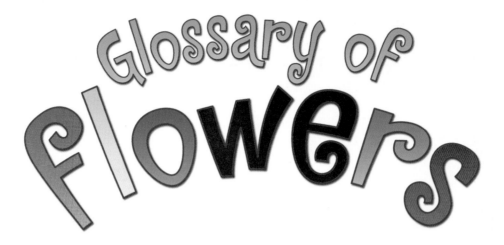

Glossary of Flowers

Just as people have nicknames that they use with family or friends, the same plant can be called a variety of things. A boy might be known as Will or Bill or Billy, and a tulip tree can also be called a yellow poplar.

But just as each of us has a formal name we were given when we were born, each plant has a name used mainly by scientists, to avoid confusion. So while a class might have two Wills, it would probably have only one William Lach. And just as there are several trees known as poplars, there is only one known as *Liriodendron tulipifera*, the scientific name for the yellow poplar or tulip tree. In the pages that follow, these formal names are listed in parentheses after the common names.

And—last thing—although some flowers can be boys or girls, most of those described in this book—like most of those in nature—are actually both male and female at the same time!

Marigold
(TAGETES GENUS)
Marigold roots are poisonous to certain nematodes, tiny worms that destroy plant roots.

Sunflower
(HELIANTHUS GENUS)

Sunflower buds turn to face the sun. After opening, the flower usually faces east, probably to protect the seeds from the hot afternoon sun.

Morning Glory
(IPOMOEA GENUS)

Morning glories open in the morning and shrivel up by afternoon. They can grow up to twenty feet a season.

Rose
(ROSA GENUS)

Roses are probably the world's most popular flower. They are famous for their beauty, scent, and thorns, although there are thornless varieties.

Hollyhock
(ALTHEA GENUS)

Hollyhocks grow up to six feet tall. A popular variety, Nigra, is maroon-black.

Snapdragon
(ANTIRHINUM GENUS)

Snapdragons can have spicy and sweet fragrances. Their dragon head–shaped flowers open their "jaws" when pinched at the back.

Daffodil
(NARCISSUS GENUS)

In the wild, daffodils often grow by the water, with the flower facing down into it. The ancient Greeks had a story that the daffodil was once a boy who liked to stare at his reflection.

Camellia
(Camellia genus)

Camellias can be as lush as roses, in a similar range of colors, although they are basically scentless in comparison.

Red Maple
(Acer genus)

Red maples bear bright red leaves in autumn, red shoots in early winter, and, in early spring, tiny red flowers that are best seen from a distance.

Cornelian Cherry
(Cornus mas)

Cornelian cherries have tiny greenish-yellow flowers in early spring, about the same time the red maple bears its flowers.

Hellebore
(Helleborus genus)

Hellebores have evergreen leaves and bloom in winter, in shades of green, pink, black, and white.

Poppy
(Papaver genus)

Poppies' brilliantly colored, crinkled petals are as dramatic as they are fleeting.

Sweet Bay Magnolia
(Magnolia virginiana)

Sweet bay magnolia flowers are usually lemon-scented. When crushed, the leaves are pleasantly scented, too.

Four-O'Clock
(MIRABILIS GENUS)

Four-o'clocks open in late afternoon or on cloudy mornings, a complement to morning glories.

Apple
(MALUS GENUS)

Apple trees bear very fragrant, honey-scented spring flowers.

Cherry
(PRUNUS GENUS)

The Japanese started festivals to celebrate and admire cherry blossoms. Cities throughout the world now hold cherry blossom festivals as a way to celebrate spring.

Prickly Pear
(OPUNTIA GENUS)

Prickly pears carry two types of dangerous spines. However, they also bear bright flowers and sweet fruit.

Azalea
(RHODODENDRON GENUS)

Every spring, azaleas are blanketed with vibrant, trumpet-shaped flowers.

Forsythia
(FORSYTHIA GENUS)

Covered with small, yellow, bell-shaped flowers and easy to grow, forsythia bushes are a common sight in many temperate climates.

Mock Orange
(PHILADELPHUS GENUS)

About three hundred years ago, Mock Orange bushes were given their common name for their highly fragrant white flowers. Large, billowing shrubs, they are less commonly planted today.

Nicotiana
(NICOTIANA GENUS)

The flowers of many Nicotiana species release a powerful fragrance on hot summer nights.

Impatiens
(IMPATIENS WALLERIANA)

Impatiens bloom reliably and repeatedly where few flowers do—in shade.

Tulip Tree
(LIRIODENDRON TULIPIFERA)

Tulip tree flowers are about the same shape and size as tulip flowers, but those on the tree are yellow-green and grow above high branches.

Franklinia
(FRANKLINIA ALATAMAHA)

Franklinia trees were discovered in the backwoods of Georgia about 250 years ago. Less than 40 years later, they could no longer be found in the wild.

Bumble Bee
(BOMBUS GENUS)

Bees and other insects, such as moths and flies (as well as birds, bats, and the wind), help most plants make seeds by visiting flowers. Flowers provide the bees with nectar, which is food for the bees, and which they turn into honey.

Grow a Flower-Friend Garden

Flowers grow most everywhere, but if you want to grow them quickly, it's best to try annuals. Annuals grow from seed in one season: Pop the seed into the ground, and about three months later, you've got a bloom!

Here are three easy gardens that contain flowers from this book: a bug-scaring garden of marigolds, a sun-loving garden of sunflowers, and a fast-growing garden of morning glories. All of the plants have big seeds that won't fall through your fingers, and all will grow just about anywhere there is sun. All can be started outdoors when the nights are warm enough to wear just a light jacket. Once they're planted, the seeds must be kept watered. How much and how often to water depends on how warm the temperature is.

A Bug-Scaring Garden

Marigold scares all the bugs. He likes to make them run.

Marigolds have unusual, needle-shaped seeds that are half black and half silver. The blooms range in color from the palest yellow to red-orange. Best of all, they have a peppery fragrance that's unlike that of any other flower. Their roots are poisonous to nematodes, which are very tiny worms that burrow into the roots of plants and weaken or kill them. Marigolds are a great plant to grow in pots or window boxes.

How to plant marigolds

1. Choose your container. Make sure it has holes in the bottom so excess water drains away.
2. Place some small rocks or broken clay-pot pieces over the holes to aid in drainage (so soil doesn't plug up the holes!).
3. Fill the container with potting soil to about one inch below the rim.
4. Drop the seeds about a finger's width apart on the surface of the soil.
5. Sprinkle just enough soil over the seeds to cover them.
6. Water thoroughly so that the water comes out of the holes in the bottom of the pot. (If the seeds appear through the soil after you water them, just sprinkle a little more soil on top until the seeds are completely covered.)
7. Keep the soil moist but not wet or muddy.

· · · · ·

After about two weeks, when the seeds start to sprout (these are called seedlings), your container will start to get pretty crowded. Pull out some of the seedlings so that the ones remaining are about a hand's width apart from one another. When the marigolds bloom, make sure you smell their distinctive, spicy scent.

When the flowers start to fade, save a few of the old blossoms and put them in an envelope. If you pull the flowers apart once they are dry, you'll find more marigold seeds, ready for planting next year!

A Sun-Loving Garden

Sunflower's big happy face basks in the morning sun.

When you look at their bright yellow petals surrounding a large, central disk, it's easy to see how sunflowers got their name. Another reason is that the bud (the flower before it opens) follows the path of the sun through the sky. After the flower opens, it usually faces east. Most sunflowers grow about three to five feet tall, but some grow even taller—the *Guinness Book of World Records* lists the tallest plant at twenty-five feet—and there are also dwarf varieties.

Sunflower seeds were a common part of the diet of many Native American peoples, and they are still grown for food today, all over the world. The large-shelled, black-striped seeds or the unhulled kernels are great for snack time. Birds, of course, love them, too.

Because of their size, sunflowers are best planted in the ground.

HOW TO PLANT SUNFLOWERS

1. Find a nice sunny spot that will get sunlight all spring and summer long.
2. Break up the dirt with a spade, in an area about the length of your hand.
3. Make a little hole in the soil with your pinkie finger, up to the first knuckle. Drop a seed in and cover it with dirt. Plant the next seed a hand's width away. When you're done, water the seeds until the earth is wet.

When the sunflowers sprout, they'll need more room to grow. There should be at least two hands' width of distance between each flower, with more space needed for the larger kinds. Pull out the sprouts in between.

Sunflowers are originally from Mexico, so in some places they grow tall without too much extra water, although that all depends on the weather where you live. Before the buds open, watch them follow the sun. After they open, they won't follow the sun anymore, but you can watch for the birds that come to nibble at them.

A Fast-Growing Garden

Morning Glory loves sun, too, and grows and grows and grows.

Morning glories get their name because they open in the morning and shrivel up by the early afternoon. They come in many colors, with the most commonly grown a variety called heavenly blue, which is the color of a morning summer sky. (A closely related flower is called moonflower, and it is pure white and opens at night.)

Morning glories don't mind if the soil isn't the best, and unless your soil is as hard as a rock, you can plant them without doing any heavy-duty digging.

HOW TO PLANT MORNING GLORIES

1. Choose a spot near a trellis, fence, or similar structure.
2. Use your finger or a spade to make a little hole in the ground. The hole shouldn't be deep at all—if you stick your index finger into the hole, your first knuckle should peek above the hole.
3. Cover the seed with soil, and plant the next seed a hand's width apart.
4. Water the seeds well when you're done—the seeds are hard and need lots of moisture to get going.

· · · · ·

When the plants start to come up out of the soil, just let them be. Morning glories do not need to be pulled to make room, unless of course you didn't follow the instructions and planted them too close!

At first, morning glories don't seem to grow very much after they pop out of the ground, but don't be fooled—once they've grown roots and the weather gets hot, they will grow a few inches a day. They twine and climb as they grow. By the end of the summer, your mornings will be a sea of blue.

If you plan to grow morning glories, make sure you like them. Once you plant them, they often replant themselves, year after year!

A Few More Things to Know About Gardening

- Botanical gardens are great places to learn about gardening. Many have fun programs, and some have greenhouses that you can explore no matter what the weather is like outside.

- Plants you find in the wild could be rare species, so it's best to buy your plants rather than collect them on an outdoor walk if you live in the country.

- It might be a good idea to ask a grown-up to help you water your garden. When things get busy, it's easy to forget to do it yourself, and if there's a hot, dry spell, the plants can die if they go without water for long. In a window box, where there's not much soil, the plants definitely can't be forgotten because they'll dry up quickly.

- Don't be afraid of bugs! Many pesky critters, like aphids, eventually attract their own enemies, such as ladybugs and praying mantises, and it's fun to watch the good guys make lunch out of the bad ones.

- No matter what pests you have, a garden is never a good place for poison. If your plants don't seem to do well, just try other kinds in a different area, or dump out your pots and put in fresh soil and different seeds.

- Whether you grow your garden on a windowsill or in a backyard, whether your plants look as neat as a supermarket or as messy as your backpack, it's your garden, so it's got to make you happy.

Happy gardening!

Artist's Note

I had a lot of fun doing this book. First I sketched the flowers and the bugs in pencil. Then I painted the flowers using acrylic paint on Arches watercolor paper and scanned them on the computer. The bugs I painted directly on the computer.

• • • • •

Special thanks to Elizabeth Peters at the Brooklyn Botanic Garden
for her assistance with photographic research.

• • • • •

Library of Congress Cataloging-in-Publication Data

Lach, William, 1968–
My friends the flowers / by William Lach ; illustrated by Doug Kennedy.
p. cm.
Summary: A bee describes his many friends, who just happen to be flowers, including prickly Rose, happy Sunflower, and shady Impatiens. Includes a brief description of each flower and instructions on how to plant a garden.
ISBN 978-0-8109-8397-7
[1. Stories in rhyme. 2. Flowers—Fiction. 3. Bees—Fiction.] I. Kennedy, Doug, ill. II. Title.
PZ8.3.L113My 2010
[E]—dc22
2009023008

Text copyright © 2010 William Lach
Illustrations copyright © 2010 Doug Kennedy

Copyright for the photographs accompanying the glossary of flowers belongs to the following:
Marigold, daffodil, camellia, cornelian cherry, hellebore, cherry, and forsythia copyright © Brooklyn Botanic Garden;
sunflower, morning glory, rose, hollyhock, snapdragon, red maple, poppy, prickly pear, mock orange, nicotiana,
impatiens, and bumble bee copyright © Laura Berman; sweet bay magnolia copyright © Kevin Gaeke; four-o'clock
copyright © James M. Hanlon; apple copyright © Darlene Martin; azalea copyright © Arjo Vanderjagt; tulip tree
copyright © Clayton Parker; franklinia copyright © Chris Hiester

Book design by Maria T. Middleton

Printed and bound in China
10 9 8 7 6 5 4 3 2 1

Abrams Books for Young Readers are available at special discounts when purchased in quantity for premiums and
promotions as well as fundraising or educational use. Special editions can also be created to specification. For details,
contact specialmarkets@abramsbooks.com or the address below.

ABRAMS
THE ART OF BOOKS SINCE 1949

115 West 18th Street
New York, NY 10011
www.abramsbooks.com